K k

Kaya's Kindergarten and the Letter K

Alphabet Friends

by Cynthia Klingel and Robert B. Noyed

The **Child's World**®

The Child's World®

Published in the United States of America
by The Child's World®
P.O. Box 326
Chanhassen, MN 55317-0326
800-599-READ
www.childsworld.com

The Child's World®: Mary Berendes, Publishing Director

Editorial Directions, Inc.: E. Russell Primm, Editorial
Director; Emily Dolbear, Line Editor; Ruth Martin,
Editorial Assistant; Linda S. Koutris, Photo Researcher
and Selector

Photographs ©: Corbis: Cover & 21, 10; Ariel Skelley/
Corbis: 9; Theo Allofs/Corbis: 13; Pat Doyle/Corbis:
14; Mark Gamba/Corbis: 17; Siede Preis/Photodisc/
Getty Images: 18.

Library of Congress Cataloging-in-Publication Data
Klingel, Cynthia Fitterer.
  Kaya's kindergarten and the letter K / by Cynthia
Klingel and Robert B. Noyed.
     p. cm. — (Alphabet readers)
Summary: A simple story about three kindergarteners
and their teacher introduces the letter "k".
  ISBN 1-59296-101-0 (Library Bound : alk. paper)
[1. Kindergarten--Fiction. 2. Alphabet.] I. Noyed,
Robert B. II. Title. III. Series.
PZ7.K6798Kay 2003
[E]—dc21   2003006616

Note to parents and educators:
The first skill children acquire before becoming successful readers is individual letter recognition. The Alphabet Friends series has been created with the needs of young learners in mind. Each engaging book begins by showing the difference between the capital letter and the lowercase letter. In each of the books on the vowels and the consonants c and g, children are introduced to the different sounds that the letter can make. Finally, children see that the letters can be found at the beginning of a word, in the middle of a word, and in most cases, at the end of a word.

Following the introduction, children meet their Alphabet Friends. The friend in each story encounters many words that include the featured letter of that book. Each noun that begins with the title letter is highlighted in red with the initial letter of the word in bold. Above the word is a rebus drawing that establishes a strong picture cue.

At the end of each book, we have included three words lists. Can your young learners find all the words in each book with the title letter in them?

Let's learn about the letter **K.**

The letter **K** can look like this: **K.**

The letter **K** can also look like this: **k.**

The letter **k** can be at the beginning of a word, like kids.

kids

The letter **k** can be in the middle of a word, like package.

pac**k**age

The letter **k** can be at the

end of a word, like desk.

des**k**

Kaya goes to kindergarten. Kenneth is

in her class. There are many other kids

in kindergarten.

Ms. Kline is the **k**indergarten teacher.

She keeps the **k**ids busy in class.

Ms. Kline is kind to the **k**ids.

Ms. Kline is teaching **K**aya about

kangaroos. **K**aya has a book about

kangaroos in her backpack.

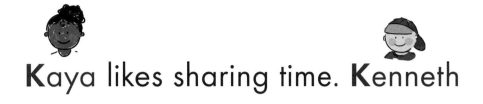

Kaya likes sharing time. **K**enneth

shows the class his **k**ittens. **K**aya

wants to keep one of the **k**ittens.

Kaya likes gym class. They are learning

karate. **K**aya likes to kick in **k**arate.

After **k**arate, it is snack time. **K**aya

likes to drink juice and eat crackers.

Kindergarten is done for the day.

Ms. Kline waves goodbye to the **k**ids.

Kaya loves **k**indergarten!

Fun Facts

The **k**angaroo is a type of furry animal that hops on its hind legs. Adult male **k**angaroos are about 6 feet (1.8 meters) tall and can weigh up to 198 pounds (90 kilograms). But a baby **k**angaroo, called a joey, is only about 1 inch (2.5 centimeters) long at birth and weighs about 0.03 ounce (1 gram). That means a newborn **k**angaroo is about as heavy as a paper clip! A mother **k**angaroo carries its baby in a pouch on her belly until the joey is about one year old.

*K*arate is a Japanese word meaning "empty hand." **K**arate is a form of combat in which the only weapons are the hands, elbows, knees, and feet. **K**arate was probably first used by monks in India more than 2,000 years ago. They needed a way to defend themselves against wild animals. Nowadays, **k**arate is a popular sport and a means of self-defense. Students of **k**arate are given different color belts as they improve their skill. **K**arate experts wear black belts.

To Read More

About the Letter K

Flanagan, Alice K. *Kids: The Sound of K.* Chanhassen, Minn.: The Child's World, 2000.

About Kangaroos

Carle, Eric. *Does a Kangaroo Have a Mother Too?* New York: HarperCollins, 2000.

Mayer, Mercer. *What Do You Do with a Kangaroo?* New York, Four Winds Press, 1973.

Murphy, Stuart J., and Kevin O'Malley (illustrator). *Too Many Kangaroo Things to Do!* New York: HarperCollins, 1996.

About Karate

Leary, Mary. *Karate Girl.* New York : Farrar, Straus and Giroux, 2003.

Simmons, Alex, and Alex Tiegreen (illustrator). *Karate Kids Grounded for Life?* Mahwah, N.J.: Troll Communications, 2002.

Simmons, Alex, and Alan Tiegreen (illustrator). *Karate Kids Want to Win!* Mahwah, N.J.: Troll Communications, 2002.

Words with K

Words with K at the Beginning

kangaroos

karate

Kaya

keep

keeps

Kenneth

kick

kids

kind

kindergarten

kittens

Kline

Words with K in the Middle

backpack

crackers

like

likes

package

Words with K at the End

backpack

book

desk

drink

kick

look

snack

About the Authors

Cynthia Klingel has worked as a high school English teacher and an elementary teacher. She is currently the curriculum director for a Minnesota school district. Cynthia Klingel lives with her family in Mankato, Minnesota.

Robert B. Noyed started his career as a newspaper reporter. Since then, he has worked in communications and public relations for a Minnesota school district for more than fourteen years. Robert B. Noyed lives with his family in Brooklyn Center, Minnesota.